PZ
7
.P 753
T 4
Politi
Three stalks of corn

TWO WEEK RESERVE:
NO RENEWAL

DATE DUE

Three Stalks of Corn

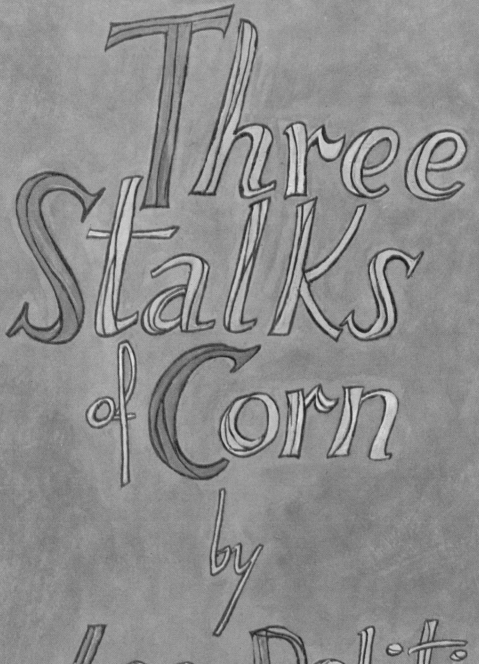

Three Stalks of Corn

by

Leo Politi

Library of Congress Catalog Card Number 75-35009
1 3 5 7 9 11 13 15 17 19 RD/C 20 18 16 14 12 10 8 6 4 2
ISBN 0-684-14572-3

Charles Scribner's Sons

ngelica lives with her grandmother in the city of Pico Rivera in California. The section of the city in which they live is the "Barrio de Pico Viejo," the district of Old Pico. Many of the people who live here are of Mexican descent.

The neighbors call Angelica's grandmother Mrs. Corrales, but Angelica calls her *abuelita,* which means "grandmother" in Spanish.

On weekdays grandmother walks Angelica to school and meets her for the walk home when school is over.

Angelica and her grandmother live in an early California house with a veranda all across the front. A large tree shades the yard, and at the bottom of the tree trunk is a statuette of the Virgin of Guadalupe—the patron saint of all Mexico.

In front of the house is a vegetable garden where grandmother grows lettuce, tomatoes, and pepper plants. She also grows patches of parsley, coriander, onions, and

garlic to flavor her food. Grandmother is a very good cook, and when she is cooking, the aroma makes everyone who smells it very hungry.

At the corner of the house grow three stalks of corn. When grandmother walks by them she stops, caresses them, and whispers:

"*¡Qué bonito!*"

"How nice!"

Angelica asks her grandmother why she loves the plants so much and she explains: "Corn is very precious to our people. It is the basis of much of our food. No part is thrown away—even the husk is used to wrap and steam the good *tamales* in. And with the corn silk we make a delicious tea."

On Saturday morning Angelica helps her grandmother prepare breakfast. They decide to have buttered *tortillas* and hot chocolate. Angelica makes the hot chocolate. With a *molinillo,* a little mill, she whips it to a foam. Angelica watches grandmother very carefully as she prepares the *tortillas.*

First grandmother grinds the corn on a stone. The grain is soft because it has been soaked in lime water during the night, so it quickly grinds into a paste. Grandmother takes a little ball of paste and pats it into the shape of a thick pancake. Angelica takes a little ball of paste also, and as they pat they hum a song.

They place the *tortillas* on an iron griddle to bake and soon a pleasant odor fills the kitchen.

"Umm!" cries Angelica as they sit at the table and eat the warm buttered *tortillas* and drink the hot chocolate.

"When I was a little girl like you, Angelica," says grandmother, "my mother taught me how to make *tortillas* just as I am teaching you, and someday you will do the same with your children."

"Will you tell me more about when you were a little girl in Mexico, *abuelita?*" asks Angelica.

"I will tell you a wonderful old legend that my mother used to tell me," her grandmother says, and Angelica cuddles close as she begins the story.

"Long long ago, when a great flood swept over the land, a little girl and boy climbed to the top of a mountain where they were safe from the flood waters. They were Tarahumares, the ancient tribe of Indians who lived and still live in that region of Mexico. When the waters subsided they came down from the mountain to find that they were the only survivors and the land that had been covered by the waters was a wasteland. They had brought with them from the mountaintop three types of corn—hard corn, soft corn, and yellow corn—the same varieties found in that part of the country today.

"The earth was moist and soft after the flood. The boy and girl planted the corn, and just a few days later corn plants sprouted from the earth and grew into tall stalks over the land. The proud plants swayed in the mountain breeze, and the golden leaves sparkled in the sunlight.

"Then they harvested the corn for food, and they lived and flourished there over many years. The Tarahumares Indians believe that they are descendants of these two survivors of the great flood."

As grandmother finished her story she looked out the window at the graceful corn stalks in her own yard.

"Corn has been the theme for many old legends," she told Angelica. "Another one that I heard from my mother many times tells of Quetzalcoatl, the mighty ruler of the Toltecs. Quetzalcoatl means The Plumed Serpent. Quetzalcoatl was also called the lord of the sky and the wind. Like all other old cultures of this continent the Toltecs knew the importance of corn. All the wise men were searching for it. But as the legend tells, it was Quetzalcoatl who first found it hidden in the hills of Tonacatépetl. Only the ants knew the way, so Quetzalcoatl transformed himself into a giant black ant and followed a queen red ant who showed him the way to the sacred hill of corn."

hen Angelica had finished her breakfast she went to play with the prized collection of tiny old corn-husk dolls that her grandmother kept on the dresser in her bedroom. Angelica loved the dolls very much, especially the puppet of a funny old witch that hung by a string from a beam on the ceiling. Sometimes grandmother would take the puppet off the hook and make it dance while she mimicked the weird sound of a witch's voice. And as the witch did her broom dance, flying and diving over the other dolls, she sang:

You have a donkey to ride on the ground,
I have my broom to take me around.
I swoop over mountains into the sky,
Oh, what fun to be a witch that can fly!

The irritated old man grumbled, the dog barked, and the donkey hee-hawed. It sounded so real to Angelica but she knew all the time it was grandmother mimicking the voices and sounds.

Grandmother knew how much Angelica liked the dolls and she decided that some day she would give them to her.

Soon after breakfast grandmother took an ear of dried corn from a basket and began to shell it.

"See, Angelica," she said, "the kernels sparkle like golden beads."

Some were yellow, others white, red, brown, and black. She punctured a hole through each kernel and then showed Angelica how she could string them together and make herself a necklace.

First Angelica took a yellow kernel, followed by a white, then a red, a brown, and a black one. As she worked the neighbor's cat came for a visit, resting his head on her foot. Soon he began to purr and take a nap. Angelica repeated the pattern until it became a lovely necklace. When she tried it on she liked it so much she asked grandmother if she could make more of them for her friends in school.

Angelica became very excited one day when she learned that a fiesta was going to take place in the little Pico Viejo Park. Because of her reputation for good cooking her grandmother was asked to be responsible for a booth at the fiesta where she would cook and sell food.

In other booths toys, fresh fruits, Mexican candies, and fruit drinks would be sold. Colorful paper streamers were hung from all the booths as everyone joined in to get ready for the festivities.

Early on the day of the fiesta, grandmother and Angelica went to the park to prepare and cook *tacos, enchiladas,* and other delicious dishes.

Everyone came to the fiesta. As people entered the park they knew that Mrs. Corrales was there cooking because they recognized the same good aroma they smelled when they went by her house.

Angelica's teacher and school principal arrived. They stopped to greet Angelica and bought some of Mrs. Corrales's *tacos.*

"These are the best *tacos* I have ever eaten," exclaimed the principal. He and the teacher were both very proud of Angelica for helping her grandmother make and serve such delicious food.

What the children liked best were Mrs. Corrales's
buñuelos. As each fresh batch was ready, the children
lined up eagerly to buy and eat them.

Buñuelos are like thick crisp *tortillas*. The dough is made with eggs and honey, spiced with paprika, and cooked in a deep fryer. *Buñuelos* are sometimes called "The Shepherds' Food." This is because during the Christmas season when the play *The Shepherds* is performed in the public square or on the streets, hot *buñuelos* are served to the actors between performances to warm them up.

One day soon after the fiesta, something very special happened at school. The principal came to see Angelica's teacher. He had been thinking about the delicious *tacos* at the fiesta.

"I think we should have a class where boys and girls can learn to cook good Mexican food as Angelica does," he said. "I have decided to ask Angelica's grandmother to teach the class."

Now grandmother did not have to return home when she walked to school with Angelica.

At school each day Mrs. Corrales taught the children new things. First, they learned to make *tortillas* well, because *tortillas* are the base for all the dishes they would learn to prepare. Soon the class was filled with the sound of patting hands and voices humming in unison a lovely song:

Chatting, singing, and laughing,
To the beat of our busy hands clapping,
Slap, slap, slap, pat, pat, pat.
Chatting, singing, and laughing,
Making *tortillas* for you and me.

In the following days the class learned to make *tacos* and *enchiladas*. Mrs. Corrales carried to school a basket of fresh vegetables and herbs from her garden to use in her cooking. She told the children that a *taco* is a *tortilla* filled with chopped meat, folded in half, and then fried crisp. Tomatoes, lettuce, onions, and grated cheese are then added. An *enchilada* is a *tortilla* filled with meat, cheese, or chicken, and then rolled, covered with chili sauce, and sprinkled with grated cheese.

Mrs. Corrales allowed each child to share in the cooking. One sliced the tomatoes, another grated the cheese, another shredded the lettuce. The boy who chopped the onions had tears in his eyes. Angelica, who already knew many things about cooking, helped the other children.

The children loved Mrs. Corrales's class because they found out they liked to cook, and also because at the end of the class they could eat the food they had made. There wasn't much of it because there were so many children to share it with, but the little they had always tasted so good. And of course the principal often visited the class and they had to share the food with him too.

When Angelica and her grandmother returned home from school one day, grandmother had a surprise for her. She took Angelica by the hand and led her to the dresser where the tiny corn-husk dolls were displayed, and said to her: "You have been such a good and helpful little girl, Angelica, that I am giving you all these dolls for your very own."

Angelica was very happy and excited, and when grandmother danced the funny witch and mimicked the witch's voice, she laughed and laughed.

When Angelica went to bed she could see through the window the profile of the three stalks of corn against the moonlit sky. She watched the leaves fluttering in the breeze. As she thought of all the good food and other things made of corn she understood why her grandmother loved her corn plants so much.

Yes, and Angelica thought of her grandmother too and of how much she loved her.

Before Angelica fell asleep, grandmother gently covered her and whispered:

"Buenas noches, Angelica." "Good night, Angelica."
Angelica replied:
"Buenas noches, abuelita." "Good night, grandmother."

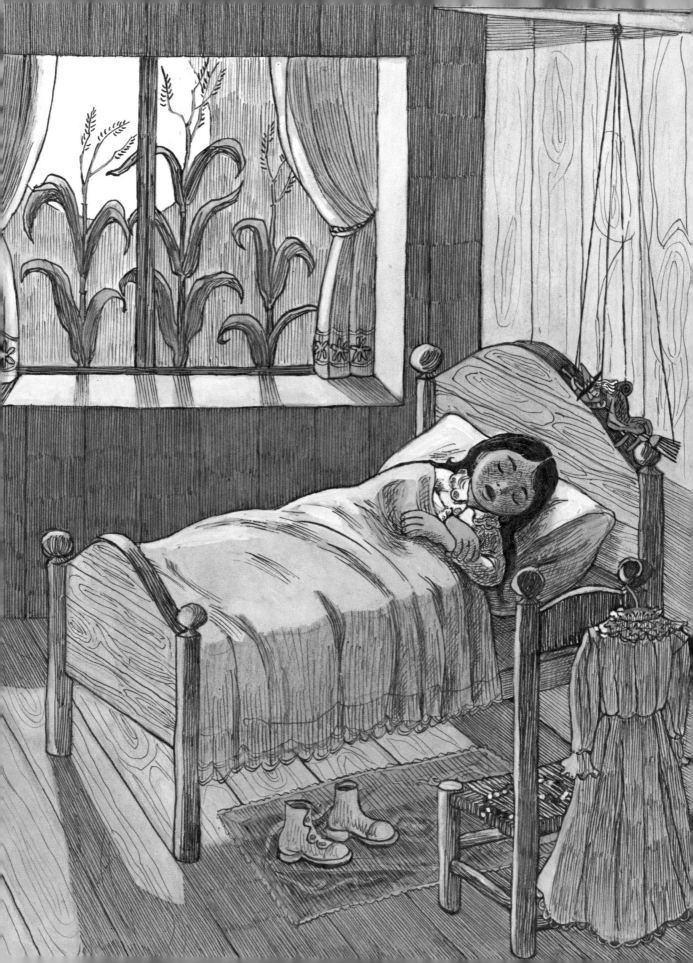

ENCHILADAS

Filling
for 12 tortillas
- 1 pound ground beef
- 1 teaspoon salt
- 1 large onion, chopped
- 1 clove garlic, finely chopped
- 1 tablespoon chili powder
- 1 cup chopped black olives
- 1 cup grated cheese

(filling may also be made of chicken or shredded beef, if preferred)

Prepare filling by frying ground beef with salt, onion, garlic, and chili powder until meat is browned. Cover bottom of a 9"x13" baking dish with ¾ cup chili sauce. Fry each tortilla briefly in hot oil to soften. Place about ⅓ cup filling on each tortilla, roll up, and place seam-side-down in baking dish. Pour 1-¼ cups chili sauce over enchiladas; sprinkle with the cheese. Bake 20 to 25 minutes at 375°F.

TACOS

Filling
for 12 tortillas
- 1 pound ground beef
- 1 teaspoon salt
- 1 large onion, chopped
- 3 tablespoon chili sauce

(filling may also be made of chicken, pork or shredded beef)

Prepare filling by frying ground beef with salt and onion until meat is browned. Add chili sauce and simmer 10 to 15 minutes. Heat tortillas on griddle to soften. Place about ⅓ cup filling on each tortilla, fold in half, and fasten with toothpick. Fry in skillet with very hot oil until crisp. Remove and drain on paper towels. Partially open the tacos and add shredded lettuce, diced tomato, and grated cheese. If desired, chopped black olives, chopped onion, and chili sauce may also be added.